Songs of Shiprock Fair

by **Luci Tapahonso**

illustrated by **Anthony Chee Emerson**

KIVA
PUBLISHING, INC.

Publisher's Cataloging-in-Publication
(Provided by Quality Books, Inc.)

Tapahonso, Luci, 1953-
    Songs of Shiprock Fair / by Luci Tapahonso;
illustrated by Anthony Chee Emerson. — 1 st ed.
    p. cm.
    LCCN: 99-63989
    ISBN: 1-885772-11-4
    SUMMARY: A young Navajo girl enjoys every part
of the annual Shiprock Fair, including the dances,
parade, carnival, exhibits, contests, food, and
the chance to visit with relatives.

    1. Navajo Indians—New Mexico—Shiprock-
Juvenile poetry. 2. Shiprock (N.M.)—Juvenile
poetry. 3. Fairs—New Mexico—Shiprock—Juvenile
poetry. I. Emerson, Anthony Chee. II. Title.

PZ8.3.T147Son 1999   [E]
               QBI99-847

Design by Rudy Ramos
Cover design by Bob Jivanjee
Art Photography by Dale W. Anderson, Aztec Media

Printed in Hong Kong

9 8 7 6 5 4 3 2 1

8-99/5M/ 1999

Kiva Publishing,
21731 E. Buckskin Drive, Walnut, CA 91789

Nezbah wakes early on Friday morning.
The sun is shining through the kitchen window
where her mother is humming an old Navajo song
as she makes breakfast. Nezbah is excited;
there is no school today. It is the first day
of the Shiprock Fair. "I can't wait to go
to the fair, Shimá, my mother," she says,
"Are our relatives coming today?"
"Yes," her mother says, "eat now so we can leave."
She smiles at Nezbah's bright eyes and excited face.
Nezbah's brother, Kiinééz, is playing basketball outside.
He shoots hoops every chance he gets.

Nezbah and her family live in Shiprock
where everyone prepares for the fair each year.
Children work on art projects for the school contests,
4-H members groom their animals for the competitions,
high school students finish sewing entries
for the Home Economics exhibits, and school bands
practice marching songs during the lunch period each day.
As artists and jewelers put the final touches on their entries,
they sing for each piece of jewelry or each painting.
At various schools, parents, relatives, grandparents,
and teachers work into the evenings building and decorating
floats for the parade. Navajo songs from radios drift
through the air as they talk and laugh.

Throughout Shiprock, people prepare for the fair.
Those who will sell food, jewelry, pottery, and other items
set up their booths and tables alongside the roads.
Music drifts through the air, and people hope
for a bit of rain so it won't be too dusty.
The scents of fry bread, stew, and roasted mutton
rise from outdoor grills. It makes everyone hungry.
The smell of strong, fresh coffee mingles
with the noises of passing cars, country music,
sizzling fry bread, and children begging for candy.
The whole town brims with excitement.
It is almost time for the Shiprock fair.

Nezbah, Kiinééz, and their father walk to the fields
each morning to see if any of the squash, melons, or
other produce can be entered in the agricultural exhibits.
They won three blue first-place ribbons the year before.
Nezbah's grandfather said it is because they are "Tóhnii,"
which means the people who live in the farm area.
The San Juan river brings them good luck.
Nezbah is proud to be a Tóhnii, especially when people
from all over the reservation compliment them on the
plentiful harvest. Their father tells Nezbah and Kiinééz
that they must remember the planting and harvest songs.

Before the fair begins, Nezbah's grandparents take them
to the Yéibicheii dances. The Yéibicheii dancers
symbolize the Holy Ones, who come each year to offer
thanks for the abundant harvest, for good health,
and for strong families. Nezbah and her grandparents
take bread, stew, flour, or coffee to the dancers.
They do this because one uncle leads a dance group
and another uncle is dancing in the sacred harvest ceremony.
The children and their grandparents stay late into the
evening. Nezbah takes a jacket and a thick blanket,
as it becomes cold after sunset. As they watch the Yéi
dance, Grandpa explains the songs to Nezbah and Kiinééz.
Nezbah sits wrapped in blankets and watches
the fire smoke rise in the cold, clear air.
They watch the dancers' feet move in smooth,
even steps on the flat, hardened ground.
Nezbah likes the lilting songs; they drift to
the bright stars far away. As they watch, Grandpa
tells Nezbah and Kiinééz to stay awake.
"You'll get your blessings if you are awake,"
he says. When Grandpa and Grandma take Nezbah
and her brother home, Nezbah is sleepy and happy.

Nezbah's aunts and uncles who live far away visit during the fair. They camp in Nezbah's family's yard. Nezbah and Kiinééz like to play with their brothers and sisters. They go to the parade, carnival, and fairgrounds together. It is fun to have so many people at the house, and to see their uncles and aunts, who always make Nezbah and Kiinééz feel very special.

On Friday night, all the children and some of the parents
go to the carnival. It is very noisy; people on the
scary rides scream, carnival workers yell out prizes,
the rides play loud music, and teenagers gather
in little groups and laugh. Nezbah likes the bright lights,
and the rides that swerve, dip, and spin quickly.
Her auntie buys her a cotton candy, and then she gets
on "The Hammer" with an older sister. She screams loudly
and holds tightly onto the bar and her sister's hand.
Her throat is a bit sore afterwards, but it's okay.

At the top of the ferris wheel, Nezbah shows her
cousin-sister the Shiprock peak in the distance.
In the cold moonlight, Shiprock is dark and large.
They wave and shout, "Shimá, my mother."
Long ago Shiprock rescued the Navajos from floods.
They wave and laugh in the clear night air
as the ferris wheel pauses above the fairgrounds;
they see the long line of carlights on the highway below,
they see the small fires at the Yéibicheii dance,
they see the thin, shiny river to the north,
and above them is the bright, round harvest moon.
Nezbah and her sister laugh and wave
as the ferris wheel glides to the ground.

On Saturday, everyone wakes at sunrise
because the parade takes place this morning.
They dress in their finest traditional clothes.
Nezbah wears a biił, a rug dress, a concho belt,
and kénitsaaí, high topped moccasins.
They eat breakfast hurriedly, then pack the cars
and pickups with chairs, blankets, and umbrellas.
Grandma and the aunties will sell coffee and donuts,
so Nezbah's father loads up the pots, cooking stove,
cups, and boxes of donuts. Finally, they leave the house
in a caravan of cars and pickups. They all follow Nezbah's
father, and he finds a good place to watch the parade.
Even though it is just after dawn, there are many families
already settled in along the parade route. While the adults
set up chairs and prepare coffee, Nezbah and the other
children sleep in the cars until the sun comes up.

When the parade begins, everyone moves to the street.
The bands play loudly, and Nezbah feels the ground
shiver with the loud drums. The sun is bright now,
and the adults take out umbrellas. The children wait
to catch candy. Their mother is happy when Nezbah
catches a bag of onions. There are powwow dancers,
country line-dancers, Pueblo and Apache dancers,
and clowns on bicycles and driving little cars.
People buy coffee and donuts from Grandma.
Nezbah sees some friends from school.
Many of the people in the parade sing Navajo songs
and dance traditional dances. Nezbah is happy
amidst all the noise and excitement.

When the parade is over, it is hot.
The families load everything and join the long lines
of cars that lead to the fairgrounds.
Nezbah, Kiinééz, and the other children go
to the carnival again with some teenage cousins
while their parents watch the afternoon rodeo.
They meet later and walk to the exhibit hall
where Nezbah's father has paintings on display.
They are happy to see that he was won two blue ribbons.
Nezbah's father smiles and doesn't say anything.
Nezbah hugs him and holds his arm for a long time.

Then they go to the powwow where Nezbah watches
the Plains Indian girls dance with light, quick steps.
Their pretty shawls sway. Nezbah likes the way
the sunlight sparkles off their dark hair and beaded jewelry.
They go to the arena where the Navajo social dances
are being held. Nezbah and her father register.
Her mother pins their entry numbers on them.
Nezbah's mother is glad that Nezbah's dress is still clean.
Nezbah and her father dance. She is proud of her father;
he is wearing a tall black hat, silver belt, and a shiny
velvet shirt. Nezbah likes the sound of the drums
and the fast songs that make the dancers turn quickly,
without any notice. Her father misses one turn.
Nezbah and Kiinééz tease him afterwards.

They dance to eight songs and then leave because
there is still much to see at the Shiprock fair.
They watch the baby contest and then watch
the men's fry bread cooking contest.
Kiinééz is surprised at how good their bread is.
The men are laughing and teasing each other.
Nezbah's mother wants to look at jewelry
and so they walk slowly between the long rows of tables
that are filled with turquoise and silver jewelry,
beautiful woven rugs and sash belts, handpainted pottery
and household items, moccasins, traditional clothes,
and much more. Nezbah's mother and grandmother
buy a necklace, two bracelets, and a ts'aa', a wedding basket.
They also buy roasted corn, which Nezbah eats right away.
It is sweet, warm, and moist.
Nezbah's grandfather buys four nitsidigo'í,
kneel-down corn bread, which he wants to save for breakfast.
But he buys coffee and eats two, then gives the rest
to children who are playing nearby.

It is now early evening, and the family goes home
to change clothes and prepare for the Yéibicheii dance.
It is the last night and the most important night
of the ceremony. They will stay until early morning, so
they take chairs, blankets, jackets, and bottles of water.
When they arrive at the Yéibicheii, they find a relative's
food booth, and eat supper. The stew is hot and tasty,
and Nezbah's mother lets her drink a cola even though
it is evening. Nezbah likes the smell
of her parents' coffee. She shares a large, crispy
fry bread with her little cousin-sister.

The family stands together in the large crowd
and watches the Yéibicheii dance. Her mother is wrapped
in a blanket. Nezbah squeezes inside the blanket
so that only her face shows. After each dance, people leave
to get coffee and Nezbah and her parents move closer
to the front of the crowd. Her father and Kiinééz
bring the chairs, and their mother, aunts, and both grandmas
sit down. Nezbah sits on her mother's lap sometimes.
Finally they move to the front, close to a fire,
and Nezbah sits on the ground, wrapped in a blanket.

Whole families watch the Yéi dance, and above them,
the moon moves slowly across the clear, cold sky.
They listen as the Yéi sing the low harmonious songs.
They watch their evergreen branches sway back and forth.
They watch the flames of the fire flicker as the Yéi prays.
They watch and know that the Yéi have blessed them again.
Nezbah and her family sit and watch until the last Yéi
has danced. It is early morning. The moon is glowing
in the west above the Carriso Mountains.

After the Yéibicheii go into their house,
Nezbah's father, brother, and uncles carry the chairs
and blankets to the pickup. Nezbah's eyes sting
from the smoke, and she is tired. She and Kiinééz
fall asleep on the way home.

As Nezbah's father carries her into the house,
he says, "Nezbah received her blessing again.
She's all worn out from the Shiprock Fair."

The Shiprock Fair is over.
The Yéibicheii have returned to their sacred home.
The children are sleeping; they dream of parade candy,
carnival rides, the Yei dancing, they dream of all their
relatives being together; they are laughing and eating.

Nezbah is sleeping.
She is smiling.
She is dreaming of the next Shiprock Fair.

About the Author

LUCI TAPAHONSO is originally from Shiprock, New Mexico and is a professor of English and American Indian Studies at the University of Arizona. She is the author of two children's books and five books of poetry, including *Blue Horses Rush In*, which was awarded the Mountains and Plains Booksellers Association's 1998 Poetry Award. Other honors include the 1998 Kansas Governor's Arts Award and "Distinguished Woman" awards from the National Association of Women in Education and the Girl Scout Council. Tapahonso was featured on Rhino Records' CD "In Their Own Voices: A Century of American Poetry" and in three films, "The Desert Is No Lady," "Art of the Wild," and "Woven by the Grandmothers: An Exhibition of 19th Century Navajo Textiles," which were released on PBS stations.

About the Illustrator

ANTHONY CHEE EMERSON lives in Kirtland, New Mexico. His mother and brother are also artists, and his children have recently begun to paint. He has recently opened his own art gallery, Emerson Gallery, in Farmington, New Mexico. He divides his time between his commercial painting business and fine art. His paintings, which have won numerous awards, have been purchased for major museum collections as well as by prominent collectors. He has also illustrated another children's book, *How the Rattlesnake Got Its Rattle*.